The Pony-Mad Princess

Princess Ellie Saves the Day

Her words made Ellie think carefully. She didn't want to get George into trouble if there was nothing wrong. But if there was, she wanted to make sure the ponies were safe. Surely there was some way they could discover the truth.

Look out for more sparkly adventures of
The Pony-Mad Princess!

The Pony-Mad Princess

Princess Ellie Saves the Day

Diana Kimpton

Illustrated by Lizzie Finlay

USBORNE

For Heather, with love – LF

This edition first published in 2014 by Usborne Publishing Ltd.,
Usborne House, 83-85 Saffron Hill, London EC1N 8RT, England.
www.usborne.com

First published in 2006. Based on an original concept by Anne Finnis.
Text copyright © 2006 by Diana Kimpton and Anne Finnis.
Illustrations copyright © 2006 by Lizzie Finlay.

A CIP catalogue record for this book is available from the British Library.

ISBN 9781409566052 JFMAM JASOND/14 01432/2

Printed in Chatham, Kent, UK.

Chapter 1

"Eighteen to me – seventeen to you," announced Princess Ellie, as she wrote the scores on the blackboard in the tack room. "I'm winning."

"Only for a bit," said her best friend, Kate. "I haven't had my turn yet."

"Here's your question," said Meg, the palace groom. "What's the name of the soft

part on the bottom of
a horse's foot?"

Kate grinned. "That's
easy. It's the frog."

Ellie changed the
score. "Eighteen all.
We're level now."

Meg peered
out of the window.
"The rain's stopped
and it's getting late.
We'd better make
this the last round of the quiz."

"Make it a hard one," said Ellie.

"I'll have to," Meg replied. "You've both
got all the questions right so far." She
paused thoughtfully for a moment. Then she
asked, "Suppose you found a pony kicking at

Kate Ellie
1 18

his stomach and looking round at his sides with a worried expression. What would be the matter?"

"Colic," cried Ellie.

Meg nodded. "And for an extra mark, what should you do?" she asked.

Ellie hesitated. She'd never seen a pony with colic and she hoped she never would. If she did, she knew she'd ask Meg for help, but that obviously wasn't the answer to the question. "I think I'd call the vet," she suggested.

"That's very sensible," replied Meg. "Colic can be serious – you don't want to take any chances."

This time Kate updated the score. "You've got twenty now. If I get both parts of my question right, it'll be a draw."

Meg handed her a few small pieces of something grey. "Do you know what this is?"

Kate stared at the pieces carefully. She rolled them between her fingers and held them up to her nose to smell them. "Is it sugar beet?" she asked.

"That's right," said Meg. "Now for that extra mark, can you tell me what you must always do to sugar beet before you feed it to a pony."

"I know, I know," squealed Ellie. She could hardly resist blurting out the answer.

"Don't tell me!" ordered Kate. She

tapped thoughtfully on her teeth with a fingernail. She stared at her feet and then at the ceiling. She stared at the blackboard, as if she was hoping the answer would miraculously appear on it. Eventually she admitted, "It's on the tip of my tongue, but I can't remember."

"Don't worry," said Meg. "Let's see if Ellie really knows."

Ellie felt very pleased with herself. "The sugar beet's been dried, so you have to soak it for a long time before you feed it to ponies."

"Of course," cried Kate. "How could I forget *that*! If you don't soak sugar beet, it might swell up inside a pony's throat and choke it."

"Well done, both of you," said Meg.

The Pony-Mad Princess

"You're the winner, Ellie, and I'm really impressed by how much you've both learned since I came to the stables."

"That's because you've taught us loads of stuff about pony care," laughed Ellie. "George never did that." George was the palace groom before Meg and Kate came. He had lots of rules, most of which began "Princesses don't..." and he never allowed Ellie to help around the stables.

"I'm glad you're here now, Meg," said Kate. "It can't have been much fun when George was around."

"And it won't be much fun if I'm told off for making you both late," added Meg. "Have you got time to check the ponies' water before you go?"

"Of course we have," said Kate. "Gran won't have my tea ready yet." Kate's gran was the palace cook.

The yard was still wet from the rain that had sent the three of them scurrying into the tack room earlier. Ellie was glad of her wellington boots as she splashed through the puddles to the tap. She filled a bucket

and used it to top up the water container in
Sundance's stable. The chestnut pony nuzzled
her shoulder as she worked. Ellie paused and
stroked his glossy neck, delighting in the
warm smell of horse mingled with the scent
of fresh straw.

Rainbow looked out of her stable to see
what was happening.
Ellie ran her fingers
through the pony's
grey mane as she
peeped over the
door to check the
water. Rainbow
hadn't touched it
yet. The container
was still full to
the brim.

Moonbeam's wasn't. It was half empty.
Ellie had to fetch another bucket to fill it up.
As soon as she'd finished, the palomino pony
plunged her creamy coloured nose into the
water and blew bubbles. Ellie laughed and
Moonbeam shook her head, tossing her
snow-white mane in all directions.

When Ellie went back outside, she saw
Kate coming out of the large stable shared
by Starlight and her foal, Angel. The other
ponies were all Ellie's, but Angel wasn't – she
belonged to Kate. "Have you checked
Shadow yet?" Ellie asked.

Kate nodded. "The silly old thing had
knocked his water over. But I've filled it
up again."

"Thanks, both of you," said Meg, as she
stepped out of Gipsy's stable. She patted

her grey thoroughbred on the neck and added, "You've saved me some work. Do you fancy a jumping lesson tomorrow?"

"That would be brilliant!" cried Ellie.

"I'll be waiting for you in the yard after school," Meg promised.

But when Ellie and Kate ran down to the stables for their lesson the next day, there was no sign of Meg at all. She had completely disappeared.

Chapter 2

"Where are you?" called Ellie. But there was no reply. Meg was nowhere to be found and all the stables were empty, too.

"That's strange," said Kate. "The ponies must still be out in the field. Meg's usually brought them in by now, especially if we're going to have a lesson."

Ellie felt a nagging fear in the pit of her

stomach. Meg had promised to be here and she always kept her promises. What could have happened to make her change her plans?

"Perhaps she's left us a message," suggested Kate. "Gran always does if she's not going to be there when I get home from school." The girls ran over to the tack room and peered inside. To their disappointment, there was no letter on the table and no message written on the board. Then Ellie noticed that those weren't the only things that weren't there. Gipsy's saddle wasn't on its rack and neither was his bridle.

She breathed a sigh of relief. "It's all right," she explained. "Meg's just gone for a ride. I expect she'll be back soon."

"I hope so," said Kate. "Let's get ready for our lesson while we're waiting."

They fetched two headcollars from the tack room and set off for the paddock.

Five of the six ponies watched them walk up to the gate. Only Shadow the Shetland took no notice. The greedy little pony was too busy eating.

They caught Moonbeam and Sundance and led them back to the yard. Then they tied the ponies up and started to groom

them. As Ellie brushed the mud from
Moonbeam's legs, she listened hopefully for
the sound of Gipsy's hooves on the palace
drive. But it didn't come.

Half an hour later, both ponies were
spotlessly clean. Kate finished painting hoof
oil on Sundance's feet and stood up. "I'm
worried," she admitted. "Meg's never been
this late before. Something must have
happened."

Princess Ellie Saves the Day

Ellie nodded in agreement. "I think we should go and look for her," she suggested.

They put on the ponies' saddles and bridles as quickly as they could. Then Ellie swung herself onto Moonbeam's back while Kate mounted Sundance. As soon as they were ready, they clattered out of the yard.

It was only when they got outside that Ellie realized how difficult their search would be. "We've no idea which way Meg went," she groaned. "She could be anywhere in the palace grounds and they're huge."

"Let's start by going up the lane," said Kate. "She nearly always goes that way and we may spot a clue or something to help us."

They rode slowly, looking carefully for any hint of Meg's whereabouts. But they didn't find one. Even if she had ridden along here, there was no way to tell if she had gone on into the deer park or turned through one of the gates.

"It's hopeless," sighed Ellie, when they reached the end of the lane. "We might as well go back. We're not doing any good out here." She tried to turn Moonbeam round to face the way they had come. But the palomino pony refused to move. Instead, she raised her head and whinnied loudly.

As the noise died away, Ellie heard another, much fainter call. Somewhere in the distance, a horse was answering. "It's Gipsy," she yelled, pointing in the direction the sound had come from. "He's over there."

"That's the end of the cross-country course," said Kate. "Let's go!"

The two girls pushed their ponies into a

gallop and raced across the open grass towards the trees that hid the wooden jumps. Normally Ellie loved riding fast, but today she was too worried to enjoy it. She leaned low over Moonbeam's neck, trying to spot Gipsy.

They found the grey thoroughbred standing all alone beside the last jump. He couldn't come to meet them – his reins were tangled in a thorn bush. "That explains why

he didn't run home," said Kate. "I wonder how long he's been here."

"And I wonder what's happened to Meg," added Ellie, her mouth dry with fear.

She jumped down from Moonbeam's back, passed the reins to Kate and walked slowly round to the other side of the jump. Skidmarks in the grass showed where Gipsy must have lost his footing as he approached the wooden poles.

At the base of the fence lay a crumpled figure. It was Meg, and she wasn't moving.

Chapter 3

"Are you all right?" cried Ellie, as she ran over to where Meg lay with one leg twisted awkwardly. She crouched down, trying desperately to remember everything she'd been taught about first aid. The only thing that came to mind was something about putting vinegar on wasp stings, or was that for bee stings? Whichever it was didn't matter.

Meg's injuries were far worse than that.

Suddenly, Meg's eyes fluttered open. "Don't move me," she whispered, in a voice so soft that Ellie could barely hear it. "Go and get help."

Ellie was relieved to be told what to do. "She needs a doctor," she shouted, as she ran back to Kate. "And it's up to us to get one."

Princess Ellie Saves the Day

"You go," declared Kate. "Moonbeam's faster than Sundance and one of us should stay here with Meg."

Ellie knew she was right, so she jumped onto the palomino's back and raced away. She went as fast as she could, galloping over the grass and slowing to a fast trot on the stony paths. As she approached the palace, Ellie spotted her parents relaxing in the garden and took a short cut towards them.

"What are you doing, Aurelia?" shouted the Queen. "You know you're not allowed to ride on the palace lawn."

"Call an ambulance!" yelled Ellie. "There's been an accident. Meg's hurt."

The King and Queen jumped up in alarm. Neither of them worried about hoofprints on the grass now. They were much too busy asking Ellie where Meg was and organizing the help she needed. Soon Higginbottom, the butler, was running to fetch the Range Rover and the wail of a distant siren announced that the ambulance was coming.

Ellie didn't ask what she should do, in case someone told her to stay out of the way. She was determined to ride back to Meg to find out what was happening. She needed to help Gipsy too. She and Kate were the only ones who knew how to look after him. It was up to them to bring him home.

She rode slowly now, giving Moonbeam time to cool down. By the time she reached the scene of the accident, the Range Rover and the ambulance were already there. Kate was standing with the King and Queen,

watching with concern as Meg was carried
into the waiting ambulance on a stretcher.
She looked pale and in pain, but she
managed to smile weakly at the girls.

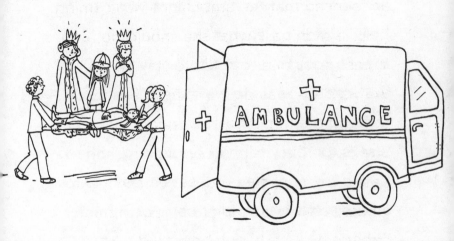

Ellie waved at her as the ambulance
doors slammed shut and the vehicle set off
on its bumpy journey across the deer park.
Then she rode over to Gipsy, jumped down
from her saddle and started to untangle the

grey horse's reins from the bush. Gipsy whickered gently and nuzzled Ellie's shoulder.

"He looks pleased to have some attention," said Kate, as she ran over to help. "I was concentrating so hard on Meg that I forgot to talk to him."

"It's a good thing we're here," said Ellie, stroking the horse's velvety neck. "Everyone else is too busy to think about him." She pulled the reins free and sorted out Gipsy's stirrups so they wouldn't bang on his sides. "I hope he'll be happy being led from Moonbeam. He's much too big for me to ride."

Ellie swung herself up into Moonbeam's saddle and tried to sort out a sensible way to hold her own reins as well as Gipsy's.

Princess Ellie Saves the Day

She had never led a horse before while
she was riding, so she was relieved that the
grey thoroughbred walked calmly beside
her when she set off. She was even more
relieved when they arrived back safely at
the stables.

The sight of the deserted yard brought
home the seriousness of what had
happened. Ellie blinked back tears as she
remembered Meg on the stretcher. Was she
going to be all right? And would she ever
be well enough to come back?

Chapter 4

Kate looked as miserable as Ellie felt.
"The stables don't feel right without Meg,"
she sighed.

"I know," replied Ellie. "I already miss her
so much." She sniffed loudly and wiped her
eyes with the back of her hand. Then she
forced herself to calm down and added,
"I'm sure Meg wouldn't want us to sit

around moping. We've got to look after the ponies by ourselves now."

They tied up Moonbeam, Sundance and Gipsy in the yard and took off their saddles and bridles. Then they set to work putting down thick, straw beds in all the stables, stuffing nets with hay and filling all the water containers.

When everything was ready, they fetched the other ponies from the field and settled them in their stables. The girls were just carrying round the feed bowls when the Queen walked into the yard.

"You are being busy," she remarked.

"We've nearly finished," said Ellie. "We've done everything all by ourselves."

The Queen smiled. "Meg would be proud of you for doing so well."

At the mention of Meg's name, Ellie couldn't hold back her tears any longer. They poured down her face as she asked, "Is she going to be all right?"

"It will be awful if she's not," wailed Kate.

"Don't worry," said the Queen, as she kneeled down on the concrete and gave both girls a hug. "Meg will be fine, thanks to your

Princess Ellie Saves the Day

rescue mission. But she will have to stay in hospital for a while."

Ellie sniffed loudly. "Can we see her?" she asked.

"Of course you can," replied the Queen. She produced a lace-trimmed hankie and dried Ellie's tears. "Your father and I are visiting her this evening, so you can come with us. The rules say only two visitors at a time, but I'm sure they can make an exception for a princess and her best friend."

An hour later, Ellie and Kate stepped out of the royal car and followed the King and

The Pony-Mad Princess

Queen into the hospital. Neither of the girls were wearing their riding clothes any more. Kate had washed away the dust of the stables and put on a white top and purple skirt.

Ellie had showered, too. She was wearing a frothy pink dress and her best tiara. In her hand, she clutched a bunch of flowers she had picked from the palace garden for Meg.

Princess Ellie Saves the Day

She had never been in a hospital before and was surprised to find it wasn't like the ones she saw on TV. There were no doctors rushing down the corridors, pushing patients on trolleys and shouting orders. The only person in the entrance hall when they arrived was a cleaner washing the floor.

"Please can you tell us the way to Buttercup Ward?" asked the King.

The cleaner looked up from his work, saw the royal family and dropped his mop in astonishment. He bowed down low and mumbled, "Third floor, on the right, Your Majesties."

The Pony-Mad Princess

Ellie and her parents stepped into the lift with Kate and pressed the button marked 3. The doors slid shut, a distant motor hummed and the lift moved slowly upwards. By the time they stepped out on the third floor, news of their visit had spread through the hospital.

The corridor was lined with staff and patients eager to see the royal visitors. Some curtseyed, some waved and some just stared with wide-eyed curiosity.

"I feel like a goldfish in a bowl, with everyone looking at me," said Kate.

"So do I," agreed Ellie. "But I'm used to it."

As they arrived in Buttercup Ward, the hospital manager rushed up. He looked flustered and was hastily straightening his tie. "Welcome, Your Majesties," he declared, as he gave a deep bow. Then he launched into a well-rehearsed speech that Ellie suspected he used on all special occasions. "It is a great honour to have you here. As a token of our esteem, please allow me to present you with..."

His voice trailed away as he realized he didn't have anything to give them. Then he grabbed a bunch of flowers from the vase by the nearest bed and thrust the dripping stems into the Queen's hands.

The old lady in the bed glowered at him. "They're mine," she grumbled.

"And very beautiful they are, too," said the Queen. She carefully put the flowers back where they belonged and dabbed her hand dry with her hankie.

The hospital manager looked embarrassed and smiled at Ellie. "It's delightful to have you here, too, Princess Aurelia."

Ellie waved her own bunch of flowers under his nose. "It's all right," she said. "I've already got some." She peered past him, spotted Meg lying on a bed in the corner of the ward and ran over to join her.

Meg looked pale and tired. Her face was scratched and one leg was in plaster.

But, to Ellie's delight, she was well enough to smile at her visitors. "Here come my rescuers," she laughed.

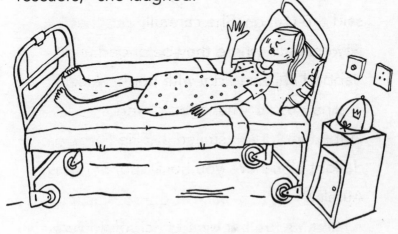

"It was Gipsy and Moonbeam who saved you," explained Kate. "We'd never have found you if they hadn't whinnied to each other."

"I'm glad Gipsy did something right," said the Queen. "Didn't he cause the accident?"

"It wasn't his fault," replied Meg. "I should have realized how slippery the ground was after yesterday's rain."

"Are you going to be all right?" asked Ellie, handing Meg the bunch of flowers.

Meg lifted them to her nose and sniffed their scent. "I already feel better now I've got these." Then she smiled and added, "Don't worry. I'm going to be fine. But I'm afraid I won't be back at the stables for a while. I've broken my leg and it will take several weeks to heal."

"You're not to worry about anything," said the King. "We can ask George to come back. Although he's retired, I'm sure he'd be happy to run the stables until you're better."

Ellie stared at her father in horror. She didn't want George to come back. She

loved being free to help out in the stables
and ride her ponies whenever she liked.
George and his rules would spoil everything.

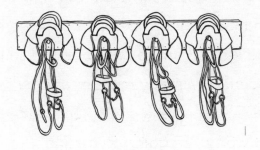

Chapter 5

"No!" cried Ellie in alarm. "We don't need George. Kate and I can look after the stables by ourselves."

The Queen shook her head. "It's too much for you to cope with. You're both too young – you can't possibly know enough."

"We do," declared Ellie and Kate

together. They both looked pleadingly at Meg. Surely she could understand why George coming back would be such a bad idea.

To Ellie's relief, Meg came to their rescue. "The girls know a great deal," she explained. "They help me all the time and I'm really impressed by the amount they've learned about pony care."

Unfortunately, the King had spotted another problem. "Looking after six ponies and a horse is hard work, Aurelia. Meg is busy all day long, but you have lessons to go to and so does Kate."

"I'll get up really early," Ellie promised.

"So will I," agreed Kate. "We can do lots of the work before school and then finish it afterwards."

"Please, please, *please*," begged Ellie.

"I'm sure we can manage, if only you give us the chance."

Her parents looked unconvinced. "I still don't think you realize how much work is involved," said the King.

"Perhaps you should let them find out," suggested Meg. She winked at Ellie and added, "It would be a very good lesson in responsibility."

The Queen patted her husband on the arm. "That's true, my dear. Responsibility is a very important thing for a princess to understand."

"I suppose so," the King reluctantly agreed. Then he turned to Ellie and said in a serious voice, "You and Kate can have your chance. But if running the stables starts to affect your school work, I will send for George immediately."

Princess Ellie Saves the Day

*

The next morning, Ellie's alarm
clock buzzed loudly at half-past
five. Ellie was already awake.
She had tossed and turned all night, thinking
of everything that had to be done at the
stables. She didn't want to make a mistake.

She pulled on her riding clothes and
raced through the silent, sleeping palace.
Her heart thumped with excitement as she
stepped outside and ran over to the stables.
This was a real adventure. She'd never been
to the yard so early before. It lay still and
quiet, waiting for the day to begin.

Sundance put his head out of his stable
and whickered a welcome. Gipsy looked
out, too. A wisp of straw clung to one of
his ears and his face looked ghostly white

in the grey light of dawn.

Kate arrived a few minutes later and the two girls set to work with enthusiasm. They started by mixing the feeds and giving them out. While the ponies munched their breakfast, the girls fetched the empty haynets from the stables and refilled them in the barn. Then they turned Gipsy and the ponies loose in the field to graze, and started mucking out the stables.

Princess Ellie Saves the Day

Without Meg's help, everything took much longer than they expected. By the time they had to go back to the palace for breakfast, they still had two stables left to clean and the yard looked a complete mess, with straw and manure all over it. But there was no time to do any more work that morning, even though they were both worried by their lack of progress. As soon as they finished breakfast, Kate had to go to school and Ellie had lessons with her governess, Miss Stringle.

The girls were used to finding everything clean and tidy when they went to the stables after school. But today was different – today the yard still looked as bad as when they'd left it. They had to finish the morning's work before they could start putting down straw beds in all the stables and refilling the water

containers. Then they had to fetch the
ponies in from the field and groom them all.

Gipsy took ages to clean up. His grey
coat was covered with stains and he wasn't
as cooperative as the ponies when they
tried to clean out his feet. Each time Ellie
picked up one of his hooves, the horse
leaned all his weight on that leg. Ellie had
to work fast, before she was forced to put
it down again.

Princess Ellie Saves the Day

There was no time to go for a ride. The whole afternoon was filled with work and, even then, they didn't manage to clean the saddles and bridles they had used the day before.

Kate sighed, as they topped up the water containers before they went home. "I never realized before how hard Meg works," she groaned. "I'm worn out."

The Pony-Mad Princess

"So am I," agreed Ellie. "I hope it gets easier once we get used to it." She felt completely exhausted. Her arms were so tired that she could hardly lift the bucket of water. She had a blister on her hand from so much sweeping and her back ached from so much lifting.

That night Ellie had no trouble sleeping. She was so tired that she didn't even dream. The problem came in the morning when she had to wake up.

Chapter 6

Ellie groaned loudly as the alarm clock buzzed. She switched it off and pulled the covers over her head. Then she remembered that she had to get up. The ponies needed her and she didn't want George to come back.

She climbed out of bed, dragged herself into her en suite bathroom and splashed cold water on her face. That helped to wake her up, so she pulled on her riding clothes and headed for the stables.

Kate was waiting for her in the yard. She was sitting on an upturned bucket, with her hair uncombed. "Are you as tired as I am?" she yawned.

"Definitely," replied Ellie, trying not to yawn too. "We'd better get started. There's loads to do."

Yesterday, running the stables had felt like an exciting adventure. Today it didn't. It was just sheer hard work – carrying feeds, filling haynets and mucking out stables. Although Ellie enjoyed taking the ponies to

the field, her aching back protested every
time she pushed the wheelbarrow, and the
blister on her hand hurt as she swept out
the stables.

The girls were so tired that everything
took even longer than it had the day before.
There was still masses left to do when they
had to go back to the palace. Ellie
considered staying longer, but she knew she
couldn't risk being late for lessons.

Back in her pink bedroom, she looked
longingly at her four-poster bed. A nap
would be wonderful, but there wasn't time.
Instead, she stood in a hot shower to ease
the aches in her muscles. Then she dressed
for lessons and ran to the dining room
for breakfast.

"Looking after the stables is certainly

giving you an appetite," said the Queen,
as Ellie started on her third slice of toast.

"Mmmm," nodded
Ellie, with her mouth
full. She'd spread
the marmalade
extra thick in the
hope it would give
her lots of energy.

The King looked at his watch. "Hurry up,
Aurelia. It's time for lessons. Remember
what I said about your school work."

Ellie didn't need reminding. The threat
of George was never far from her mind.
She gulped down the last of the toast, drank
the rest of the orange juice from her crystal
glass and ran to the schoolroom. On the
way, she sucked the stickiness of the

marmalade from her fingers – there wasn't time to wash.

Miss Stringle was already at her desk when Ellie arrived. She didn't look pleased at being kept waiting. "Sit down at once, Your Highness," she said sternly. "We'll start the morning with some mental maths to wake up your brain."

Ellie's brain was as tired as the rest of her. It didn't want to be woken up and it certainly didn't want to do maths. Although she tried hard to concentrate, she kept making silly mistakes.

"Do pay attention, Princess Aurelia," said Miss Stringle. "If one princess can kiss three frogs, how many frogs can three princesses kiss?"

Ellie wrinkled up her nose in disgust.

She didn't like the idea
of kissing frogs at all.
"Six," she guessed.

"No, no, no," said Miss Stringle. "It's
three lots of three and that is…?" She
paused dramatically, obviously waiting for
the answer.

Ellie bit her lip nervously. "Nine?" she
suggested.

"At last," sighed Miss Stringle. "Now
you've finally got one right, we'll move on
to geography." She pointed at a map of the
world pinned up on the wall. "Please point
to Andirovia and tell me about it."

Ellie stood up confidently. She knew the
answer this time because she'd been to
Andirovia to visit her friend, Prince John.
As she picked out the right place on the

map, she said, "Andirovia has lots of mountains. The weather is very different from here. In the winter, there is lots of snow."

For the first time that morning, Miss Stringle looked pleased. "Well done, Princess Aurelia. You've learned that well." She pointed at another much larger country. "Now I'm going to teach you about Sanbarosa."

Ellie sat down again, hoping the rest of the geography lesson would be as easy. To her delight, Miss Stringle switched on the television. Watching that would take no effort at all. She could do it without any problem, even though she was tired.

The television screen announced, "Sanbarosa, land of sun, sea and sheep." It was one of the most beautiful places Ellie had ever seen. A golden sun blazed down on pure, white sand. Clear blue sea lapped gently on the shore.

Ellie yawned and made herself more comfortable. Gradually, she stopped listening to the droning voice on the TV and imagined herself lying on that gorgeous beach. The more she thought about it, the more relaxed she felt. Her eyes closed, her head nodded and she fell asleep.

*

Princess Ellie Saves the Day

"Aurelia," roared the King.

Ellie woke up with a start. Her eyes snapped open and, for a brief moment, she couldn't remember where she was. Then she saw Miss Stringle and her father. They both looked very cross. "Oh dear," she groaned, as she realized what had happened.

"See?" said Miss Stringle, pointing accusingly at Ellie. "She was even snoring."

"I was not!" protested Ellie, but the King was looking at her sternly.

"Do you remember what I said would happen if running the stables affected your school work?" he asked.

Ellie nodded miserably. "You said you'd send for George."

"And I always keep my word," said the King. "He'll be here later on this afternoon."

Chapter 7

Ellie told Kate the news when they met in the yard after school. To her surprise, her friend wasn't as miserable about it as she had expected.

"I've been tired all day," Kate explained. "Looking after all the ponies is much harder than I thought. I don't think we could manage on our own until Meg comes back."

Princess Ellie Saves the Day

Deep inside her, Ellie knew Kate was right. "We do need help," she admitted. "But George will take over and stop us looking after the ponies. I'm sure he will."

Kate looked thoughtful. "Maybe he won't, if we can prove how good we are."

"I don't think that will make any difference," said Ellie. "George was very set in his ways."

"Maybe he's more relaxed now he's retired," suggested Kate. "It must be worth a try."

"I suppose so," replied Ellie, her voice tinged with doubt. She glanced round at the overflowing wheelbarrows and the untidy yard.

"Let's make sure everything is perfect when he arrives."

Their plan filled them with new energy. As quickly as they could, they finished the mucking out and put down clean straw in all the stables. Then they tied up bulging nets of hay, filled all the water containers and fetched the ponies in from the field.

Ellie was just finishing sweeping the yard when George arrived. He looked older than she remembered him. The small amount of hair on his head was grey and he walked more slowly than before. "Hello, George," she said. "We've got the ponies in for you."

The old groom smiled. "Thank you kindly, Your Highness." Then he reached out and took the broom away from her. "You won't be needing that any more. Princesses don't sweep yards when I'm in charge."

Ellie glared at him angrily. Then she glanced at Kate and whispered, "I told you so."

Kate took a step towards George. "I could do it if you like," she suggested. "I'm not a princess."

"And who might you be then?" said George.

"Kate is the cook's granddaughter," Ellie explained. "She's my best friend, too, and she owns Angel." George looked puzzled. "Who, may I ask, is Angel?"

"She's Starlight's foal," explained Ellie. She'd forgotten that so much had happened since George retired.

George raised his eyebrows questioningly. "And Starlight is...?"

"My new pony," said Ellie, proudly. "Come and meet her." She led the way to the large stable that the bay mare shared with her foal.

George looked slightly cross as he walked slowly beside her. "No one told me about extra ponies," he grumbled. "That's extra work, that is." But his face softened when he saw Starlight and Angel standing side by side, knee deep in straw. "They're beautiful, they are. That mare's a bit heavy for a princess, but she's my kind of pony."

His approval of Starlight made Ellie feel

friendlier towards him. "We'll show you round, if you like," she offered.

"I'm sure I can manage, Your Highness. I've worked here long enough to know where everything is." As if to prove his point, he marched across the yard to the feed store.

The girls followed him inside and watched as he lifted the lids on the storage bins to check what was inside. He nodded as he looked at the barley and chaff, but raised his eyebrows again when he looked into the third bin. "New-fangled nonsense," he muttered.

"It's sugar beet," said Ellie. "It's Moonbeam's favourite. But you have to soak it."

"I know, I know," said George, firmly.

"Princesses don't need to worry their heads about that sort of thing." He shut the lid, left the feed room and walked over to investigate the tack room.

Kate went to follow him inside, but Ellie stopped her. She remembered that one of George's rules was "princesses don't go in tack rooms". So the two girls stood outside and peered through the open doorway.

George muttered to himself as he looked round the room. He cleaned the blackboard, tidied a pile of pony magazines and looked disapprovingly at Moonbeam's dirty bridle. Then he turned to Ellie and asked, "Which pony would you like to ride tomorrow?"

"Rainbow," she replied. "And it's Kate's turn to ride Moonbeam."

He carefully wrote both names on the board. "Tomorrow's Saturday, and it's sensible to ride in the morning before it gets hot. I'll have both ponies ready at eleven."

"You don't have to do that," said Ellie, quickly. "Meg's taught me loads about pony care. I can get them ready myself now and I can help with the mucking out."

George stared at her disapprovingly. "There's no need, Your Highness. I can cope very well on my own. Princesses don't help at the stables when I'm in charge."

Then he glanced at Kate and added, "Neither do little girls."

Chapter 8

Ellie enjoyed being able to lie in bed the following morning. But she didn't enjoy being separated from her ponies. Usually she spent the whole of Saturday at the stables. George's arrival had changed that completely.

She met Kate in the palace garden after breakfast. They were both already in their riding clothes, although they couldn't ride until later. As there was nothing else to do until eleven, they decided to go for a walk.

"It's not fair," grumbled Ellie, as they wandered along the bank of the stream. "I'm really missing the ponies."

"So am I," moaned Kate. She threw a stick into the rushing water and watched as it was swept away. "It's silly making us book our ride instead of letting us just turn up at the stables."

"At least we can make sure it's a good ride," said Ellie. "Let's go along my favourite path in the wood – the one where the ponies splash through the stream."

"After that, let's go to the top of that hill," suggested Kate, pointing to the other side of the deer park. "I love it up there. We can have a long canter across the heather."

Planning their ride cheered the girls up. By the time they arrived at the stables, they had worked out every detail. At exactly eleven o'clock, they walked into the yard and found that George had kept his promise. He was waiting for them with Rainbow and Moonbeam. Both ponies were saddled and bridled ready to go out.

Unfortunately, they weren't the only ones. To Ellie's dismay, she noticed George had saddled Gipsy, too, and there was only one possible reason why he would do that.

"You don't need to come with us," she protested.

"Yes, I do, Your Highness," replied George. He tightened Rainbow's girth and held the pony still while Ellie mounted. "I'm the groom and that's part of my job. Princesses don't go riding by themselves when I'm in charge."

He glanced at Kate and added, "Neither do little girls." Then he helped her onto Moonbeam and fussed around, making sure her stirrups were the right length. When he was sure both girls were ready, he led Gipsy over to the mounting block and used it to swing himself onto the grey thoroughbred's back.

Ellie found it strange to see him riding
Meg's horse. "I'm surprised you didn't bring
Captain with you," she said. George had
owned Captain for as long as she could
remember and he'd taken the big, black
horse with him when he'd left the stables.

George shook his head and smiled. "It
wouldn't be fair," he explained. "My old

The Pony-Mad Princess

Captain is retired like me. He's got used to doing nothing. It wouldn't be fair to make him work hard again."

As they rode out of the yard, Ellie wondered if the same was true of George. Now she had tried running the stables, she realized what a huge amount of work there was. Maybe it was too much for one old man to manage by himself. That would explain why Rainbow still had tangles in her mane. It looked as if it hadn't been brushed at all.

The ride George took them on was not at all like the one the girls had planned. They didn't splash through the stream. They didn't ride to the top of the hill, or canter across the heather. They just walked sedately along tree-lined paths and had an occasional slow trot.

Princess Ellie Saves the Day

It was the quietest ride Ellie had been on for ages. But it was still wonderful to be on Rainbow's back, feeling the gentle rhythm of her walk and watching her flick her ears as she listened to all the sounds around them. Ellie couldn't bear the thought that this might be the only contact she had with her ponies today. She had to do something to stop George spoiling her fun.

When they got back to the yard, the two girls jumped off Moonbeam and Rainbow. George slid more slowly down from Gipsy's back. He looked stiff and tired after the ride.

Ellie spotted her chance. Before he could stop her, she led Rainbow swiftly towards her stable. "Don't worry, George," she called. "I'll unsaddle her."

She led the pony inside and looked round in surprise. Although the yard looked clean and organized, the stable didn't. Last night's haynet hung empty on the wall. Bits of hay floated in the dregs of last night's water and the floor was still covered with dirty straw and manure.

George met her at the door, as she stepped out carrying Rainbow's saddle and

bridle. He took them from her firmly,
looking slightly flustered that she'd seen
how behind he was with the work. "There's
no need for you to help," he insisted.
"I can cope. I'm just a little out of practice,
that's all."

"But we like helping," said Kate.

"That's got nothing to do with it," said
George. "Looking after the stables is my
job. It's up to me to do it." He let them
book another ride for Sunday morning.
Then he hurried them out of the yard.

"I'm worried," said Ellie, as they walked
slowly back to the palace.

"What about?" asked Kate.

"George hadn't groomed the ponies
very well," explained Ellie. "And he hasn't
mucked out the stables, either. I think he's

too old to manage on his own and, if
George can't cope, the ponies are going
to suffer."

Now Kate looked worried, too. "Perhaps
you should tell your parents," she
suggested.

Ellie shook her head. "They won't believe
me. They never do. They'll say we're
imagining it because we don't want George
to be here."

"Do you think we are?" asked Kate.

Her words made Ellie think carefully. She
didn't want to get George into trouble if
there was nothing wrong. But if there was,
she wanted to make sure the ponies were
safe. Surely there was some way they could
discover the truth.

Chapter 9

"Are you sure this is going to work?" said Kate, when the two girls met in the palace garden after lunch.

"Of course I am," replied Ellie. She held up the binoculars Miss Stringle made her use in birdwatching lessons. "We can watch George all afternoon through these to see how he's

managing. Then, if we're still worried,
I'll have some evidence for
Mum and Dad." She
looked questioningly at Kate.
"You have remembered the
notebook, haven't you?"

"Yes," laughed her friend.
"And the pencil and some
sticky buns. Gran thought
we might get hungry."

They walked up the hill overlooking the
stables and found an ideal spot. It had soft
grass to sit on, a large tree to give them
shade and a perfect view of the yard.

They took it in turns to keep watch and
write down everything they saw in the
notebook. The old groom worked slowly
but steadily all afternoon without a break.

Princess Ellie Saves the Day

He mucked out the stables, put down fresh bedding and swept the yard. By the time he fetched the ponies in from the field, he looked exhausted. His shoulders were slumped and his feet dragged as he walked.

Ellie felt sorry for him. She knew how tired he must feel. She watched until all the ponies were safely in their stables. Then she passed the binoculars to Kate while she ate the last of the buns. When she'd swallowed the last mouthful, she asked, "What's he doing now?"

"He's giving out the feeds," said Kate.

Ellie kneeled up beside her. "Can you see what he's giving them?"

"No way," said Kate. "The feed bowls are too deep. I can't see what's in them."

"I hope he's remembered Starlight's carrots," said Ellie. "She'll be miserable if she doesn't have those." The thought brought all her worries tumbling back. Watching from a distance wasn't good enough. "I can't bear not being there. I need to see for myself that everything's all right."

"So do I," said Kate. "If I don't say goodnight to Angel, she might think I don't love her any more."

They picked up the binoculars and the notebook and scurried down the hillside. Then they crept quietly up to the stables and peered into the yard.

Princess Ellie Saves the Day

"We're in luck," whispered Ellie.
George was sitting on a chair
outside the tack room.
His head was slumped forward
with his chin on his chest and
he was snoring gently.

Kate looked at the old
groom nervously.
"Maybe he's just
dozing. If he is, he'll
wake up as soon as he hears us."

"I don't think so," replied Ellie. "He
looked so tired. I bet he's fast asleep." But
she still walked on tiptoe as she led the way
into the yard.

First, they checked Sundance. The
chestnut pony flicked his ears forward when
he saw them coming and nuzzled Ellie's

shoulder. She gave him a peppermint and stroked his face.

"He looks fine," whispered Kate. "Maybe we've been worrying about nothing."

Suddenly, there was a most peculiar noise. It was a strange sort of cough, quite different from anything Ellie had ever heard before. She ran quickly to the next stable and peered over the door, searching for the source of the sound. Rainbow looked back at her, happily munching a wisp of hay. There was nothing wrong here.

The strange cough came again. This time Ellie realized who was making it. "It's Moonbeam," she cried. She raced towards the palomino pony's stable, with Kate close behind.

As soon as they opened the stable door,

they realized something was dreadfully wrong. Moonbeam looked terrified. She was standing with her head and neck outstretched. She was coughing and struggling to swallow.

"What's wrong with her?" asked Kate, her eyes wide with alarm.

"I don't know," cried Ellie. Then she glanced down at the feed bowl and spotted a few pieces of something grey and dry lying in the bottom of it.

A shiver of fear ran down her spine as she realized what must have happened. George had fed Moonbeam sugar beet, but he'd forgotten to soak it first. Now Moonbeam was in terrible danger.

Chapter 10

Ellie raced to the phone in the tack room, while Kate ran to check the other ponies. Neither of them worried about being quiet now. All that mattered was saving Moonbeam.

George woke up with start and stared crossly at Ellie. "What's happening?" he asked.

Princess Ellie Saves the Day

"We've got to get the vet," she shouted. "Moonbeam's choking on the sugar beet."

George's grumpiness immediately disappeared. "I'll call him," he said. "You go back to Moonbeam. Keep her calm and make sure she doesn't eat or drink anything."

He vanished into the tack room, and Ellie ran back to Moonbeam's stable. As her feet pounded on the yard, she repeated George's instructions to herself to help her remember them. It was only then she realized that, for the first time ever, George had asked her to help.

She found Moonbeam still looking as distressed as she had before. Ellie stroked the pony's neck soothingly. Then she quickly moved the feed bowl and water out of reach.

Running footsteps outside announced Kate's return. She slipped quietly through the door and announced, "All the others are fine. I don't think he gave them any sugar beet."

"Thank goodness for that," said Ellie. She quickly explained George's instructions. Then she stroked Moonbeam's face again and whispered, "Don't be scared. Everything's going to be all right." She tried to sound confident but she didn't feel it.

To Ellie's relief, the vet arrived a few minutes later. "It's your lucky day," he said. "I was just up the road seeing to a sick cow."

He opened a bag and gave Moonbeam an injection. "That will make her relax so it's easier for the sugar beet to go down." Then

he pulled a long
bendy tube from
his bag and explained:
"I'm going to push this
gently down her throat
and put some water
down it to clear away
the blockage."

Moonbeam already
looked calmer. Ellie
wanted to stay with her,
but the vet needed space to work. "You two
girls have done a splendid job," he said.
"But there's nothing more you can do
for the moment. I'll call you back when
I've finished."

Ellie stepped reluctantly into the yard
and was relieved to see her parents waiting

for her. They had heard there was an emergency and come immediately to find out what was happening.

The Queen gave Ellie a big hug. "Moonbeam's in good hands. The vet is a very clever man."

Ellie knew she was right, but it didn't stop her worrying. The minutes ticked by painfully slowly. The longer she waited, the more anxious she became.

Eventually, the door swung open and the vet stepped out. To Ellie's relief, he was smiling broadly. "Panic over," he announced. "Moonbeam's going to be fine."

As if to prove the point, George led the palomino pony out into the yard. She looked like her normal self again.

"Thank you, thank you," squealed Ellie, as she threw her arms round Moonbeam's neck.

"Thank *you*," laughed the vet. "It's you who spotted the problem so quickly."

"And it's me who caused it," said George, sadly. "I gave the sugar beet to Moonbeam because you said she liked it. But I was so tired that I forgot all about soaking it." He turned to the King and bowed. "I'm very sorry, Your Majesty. I'm afraid I'm too old to run the stables. I will leave immediately, of course."

Ellie felt sorry for him. He hadn't wanted to hurt Moonbeam. He'd been trying to make her happy. "You don't have to go," she said. "You could stay and let us help."

"We can't run the stables without you," explained Kate. "And you can't manage all the work without us. But together we could make a good team."

"That's an excellent idea," said the King. He turned to George and asked, "Would you be happy with that, just until Meg comes back?"

George smiled. "It sounds like the perfect solution," he replied. "Princesses seem good at helping." He glanced at Kate and added, "So do little girls."

Ellie grinned and hugged Moonbeam again. She was still looking forward to Meg coming back, but life with George was going to be much more fun from now on.

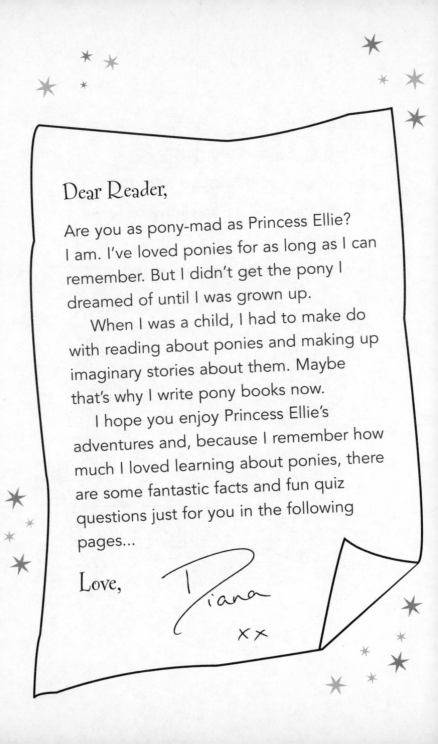

Dear Reader,

Are you as pony-mad as Princess Ellie?
I am. I've loved ponies for as long as I can
remember. But I didn't get the pony I
dreamed of until I was grown up.

When I was a child, I had to make do
with reading about ponies and making up
imaginary stories about them. Maybe
that's why I write pony books now.

I hope you enjoy Princess Ellie's
adventures and, because I remember how
much I loved learning about ponies, there
are some fantastic facts and fun quiz
questions just for you in the following
pages...

Love, Diana

x x

Pony-Mad Fun & Facts

Famous horses

Horses become famous in different ways –
some are ridden by famous people, others
are good at a particular sport, some even
appear in films...

RED RUM: This beautiful bay thoroughbred
is the only horse to have won the gruelling
Grand National race three times. He became
so famous that his death, at the grand old age
of thirty, was front-page news.

BLACK BESS: This black mare was famous for
being ridden by the highwayman Dick Turpin.
The story goes that Dick rode 200 miles on
Bess from London to York in one night. No
horse could really have made such a long
journey but that didn't stop the legend of
Black Bess!

BLACK BEAUTY: Anna Sewell's classic book *Black Beauty* is about a black horse and his life with various owners, some good and some bad. He may not have been real but his story can still make readers cry!

CLEVER HANS: This horse became famous for being able to do arithmetic. He would tap the ground with his hoof to count out the answers. Research eventually showed that he couldn't really count – he was reading the body language of his owner to work out when he should stop tapping. But that's pretty clever too.

PEGASUS: The great winged horse of Greek legend was beautiful and brave. He is usually drawn with white wings, but some versions of the story say they were golden.

TRIGGER: This palomino (originally called Golden Cloud) was a Hollywood star in the 1930s, appearing in cowboy films and TV series. He could walk up to fifteen metres on his hind legs. His owner, the film star Roy Rogers, called him Trigger because he was so quick.

Princess Ellie's Pony-Mad Quiz

Do you know your **saddle** from your **stirrup**? Do you know about **Ellie's** favourite places to ride? Test your knowledge of Princess Ellie's world with this quiz!

1. What is the name of the soft part on the bottom of a horse's foot?
a) Toad
b) Frog
c) Newt

2. What must you do with sugar beet before feeding it to a pony?
a) Chop it up
b) Sprinkle it with sugar
c) Soak it

3. What is the name of Meg's horse?
a) Gipsy
b) Gerald
c) George

4. Which of these does Ellie use as bedding for her ponies?
a) Feathers
b) Leaves
c) Straw

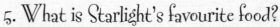

5. What is Starlight's favourite food?
a) Carrots
b) Turnips
c) Tomatoes

6. Ellie likes her favourite path through the wood because the ponies can:
a) Jump over stiles
b) Kick through the leaves
c) Splash through the stream

7. The front of the saddle is called:
a) The poodle
b) The pommel
c) The puddle

Turn the page to
find out the answers...

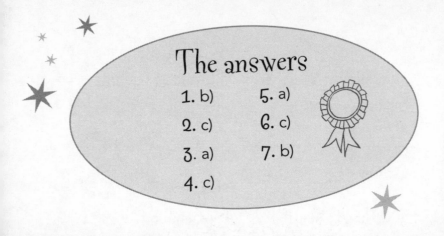

The answers

1. b)   5. a)

2. c)   6. c)

3. a)   7. b)

4. c)

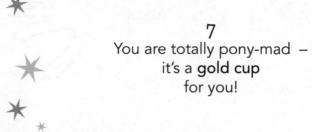

Tot up your total to see just how
pony-mad you are...

1-3
A good try.

4-6
Great knowledge and a big rosette!

7
You are totally pony-mad –
it's a **gold cup**
for you!

How to...
Look after a pony

GROOMING

As Ellie and Kate know, looking after a pony is hard work! There's lots to do every day and it's important to establish a routine so your pony can look forward to your visits.

* The most important foods for your pony are grass and hay. Only give other foods like oats or pony nuts if he really needs them.

* Turn your pony out into a field whenever possible. All ponies need time to graze and move around, and some ponies can live outside all the time. Make sure the field has good fencing, a water trough and shelter from wind and rain.

* Muck out the stable every day by removing all the droppings and dirty bedding, using a shovel or fork and a wheelbarrow.

* Put down fresh bedding when necessary. The bed needs to be deep enough to let your pony lie down without hurting himself on the hard floor underneath.

* Ponies need water available all the time so refill buckets regularly and remember to break the ice on the trough in winter.

* When you fetch your pony from the field, check him carefully for injuries and clean out his hooves to make sure he hasn't picked up any stones.

* Clean your saddle and bridle regularly to keep it supple and comfortable for your pony to wear and rinse the bit with water after every ride.

Read on for a sneak preview of
Princess Ellie's next adventure...

Chapter 1

"It looks wonderful," yelled Princess Ellie, as she stared out of the helicopter window. She had to shout to be heard above the roar of the engine.

"Fantastic!" agreed her best friend, Kate, at the top of her voice.

They both stared down, watching the tropical island come closer and closer.

Its hills were covered with thick, green jungle, and blue sea lapped gently on its white, sandy beaches. It looked like the perfect place for a summer holiday. There was only one problem – there was no sign of any ponies.

The helicopter landed gently on a patch of ground marked with an enormous H. The wind from its rotor blades sent up clouds of dust that blocked the view from the window. Then the engines finally stopped and all was quiet.

"Thank goodness," said the Queen. "That journey was too long and too noisy."

"But it was worth it, my dear," said the King. "We've got nothing to do for the next two weeks except relax and swim and make new friends."

"And ride," added Ellie. "You promised there'd be riding." She was starting to feel worried. If there weren't any ponies, her holiday would be ruined.

Before either of her parents could answer, the helicopter door swung open. "Welcome to Onataki," announced a man in a brightly coloured shirt. "Hi! I'm Don – I own the island."

Ellie and Kate followed the King and Queen out of the helicopter. The sun was so bright that it dazzled them. The air was hot and the gentle breeze carried strange scents Ellie didn't recognize.

As soon as they were all on the ground, a crowd of smiling women ran forward and hung garlands of flowers around their necks. One of them accidentally knocked the King's crown sideways, but he didn't seem to mind. He just laughed as he pushed it straight.

Kate nudged Ellie with her elbow. "Why aren't they bowing and curtseying like people usually do when they see your parents?"

"Dad says they don't bother with that here," explained Ellie. "Lots of the people who come to this island are royal. The others are all millionaires or famous film stars."

"Except me," laughed Kate. Her gran was the palace cook.

"And the maids and Higginbottom," added Ellie. She glanced back at the helicopter where the butler was busy making sure all their luggage was unloaded.

Don led the way to a white building

with RECEPTION written on it in large gold letters. Inside, full-size palm trees grew in pots and goldfish swam lazily in a huge pool.

While Don chatted to the King and Queen, the two girls looked around at the walls. There were photos of people waterskiing and sailing. There were notices about golf and fishing and tennis. But there was nothing at all about horse riding.

Ellie tugged anxiously at her mum's sleeve. "Ask about the ponies," she begged.

"In a minute, Aurelia," replied the Queen.

Ellie sighed. She knew from experience that that sort of minute often lasted several hours.

Don picked up some keys from the desk. "Come with me and I'll show you where you're staying." He led the royal group through the reception area and out the other side.

"Wow," cried Kate and Ellie together, as they stepped onto a wide, sun-soaked patio.

Straight in front of them was an enormous swimming pool with water as blue as the sky. Beyond that lay a wide, sandy beach dotted with striped sun umbrellas. And on either side of the pool stood the villas for the guests, each with its own garden.

Ellie was pleased to find their villa was at the far end, closest to the beach. It was totally different to the palace where she normally lived. It was much smaller, and it had a wide, shady veranda and a roof of green tiles. In the garden, hummingbirds flew from flower to flower and a fountain splashed gently into a shell-shaped pool.

To Ellie's surprise, Higginbottom opened the door to greet them. He was slightly out of breath from rushing to get there before they did, and his garland of flowers looked ridiculous on top of his evening suit.

He smiled at Ellie and pointed at one of the doors, leading off the sitting room. "That's your room, Your Highness. And Kate's. His Majesty thought you'd like to share."

To find out what happens next read

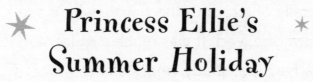

Princess Ellie's Summer Holiday

The Pony-Mad Princess